Baby Stegosaurus

By Beth Spanjian
Illustrated by Alex Bloch

MERRIGOLD PRESS • NEW YORK

The tropical forest smells damp and fresh. A young bird perches on a branch and begins preening his feathers. Hidden deep within the lush greenery below is a nest of stegosaurus eggs.

The sun's rays pierce through the trees and flood the nest. Suddenly, an egg begins to rock. Within minutes, Baby Stegosaurus pokes her head through the shell.

As she struggles from her shell, another egg begins to hatch. By noontime, the whole nest is squirming with little dinosaurs! Baby Stegosaurus fights to keep on top of the pile, as the babies crawl all over each other.

The little ones don't stay in the nest for long. Baby Stegosaurus is the first to climb out. As she waddles into the nearby ferns, two more babies follow close behind.

Baby Stegosaurus slowly makes her way through the ferns. She and her brothers nibble on the narrow leaves. Finding a sunny spot on the forest floor, Baby Stegosaurus stops to rest and warm herself.

Then the ground begins to shake. Baby Stegosaurus and her brothers scurry under some leaves.

A huge allosaurus bounds past the babies.
Fortunately, the meat-eater doesn't know
the baby dinosaurs are there.

Another stegosaurus isn't so lucky. The hungry allosaurus is heading straight for him. The adult has been peacefully eating his fill of ferns and horsetails.

Now the stegosaurus's quiet afternoon turns into a battle. The allosaurus lunges toward the plant-eater. With surprising quickness, the stegosaurus turns and lashes at the ferocious creature with its powerful tail. Its sharp spikes miss the allosaurus by inches.

The two dinosaurs battle back and forth. Every plant in their path is flattened. The allosaurus finally gives up and retreats.

Baby Stegosaurus has been standing motionless in the ferns. Instinct has told her to freeze. Now that things are quiet, Baby Stegosaurus goes back to snipping bite-sized pieces from the leaves.

Baby Stegosaurus moves from plant to plant until the cool evening air slows her down to a snail's pace. By dark, the three little dinosaurs have found a comfortable spot, where they will stay until the morning sun warms them again.

Facts About Baby Stegosaurus

When Did Stegosaurus Live?

Stegosaurus lived during the late Jurassic Period, about one hundred fifty million years ago. Stegosaurus belonged to a group of dinosaurs called the stegosaurs, which were armed with plates and spines. Stegosaurus was the largest and most heavily armored of all its cousins. Its name comes from two Greek words meaning "plated lizard."

What Did Stegosaurus Eat?

Stegosaurus ate horsetail ferns and other plants. Stegosaurus had a small mouth and weak little teeth that could tackle only the softer plants. Some scientists believe that stegosaurus wasn't limited to low-growing plants, but possessed the body and balance to push itself up onto its huge hind legs and tail to reach tender leaves up to twelve feet off the ground.

How Big Was Stegosaurus?

Stegosaurus grew up to thirty feet long and weighed up to four tons. The dinosaur stood over eight feet at the hips and sixteen feet at the top of its plates. With a brain the size of a walnut, stegosaurus wasn't the most intelligent animal of its time. To help move and control its massive hind legs and powerful tail, the dinosaur developed what is referred to as its "second brain," a large mass of nerves on its spinal cord between its hips. As for stegosaurus's plates, paleontologists (people who study fossils) have argued for years whether the two rows alternated or matched. Because the plates were not attached to the skeleton, the fossils leave no obvious signs about their arrangement. The latest theory, however, says that stegosaurus had only one row of plates.

What Was A Stegosaurus's Family Like?

Scientists know very little about the family life of a stegosaurus. Some fossils believed to be those of a stegosaurus show that the babies hatched from large, oval eggs. The fossils also show that the baby stegosaurus may not have had plates along its back. Until more evidence is uncovered, no one really knows whether stegosaurus traveled in herds or cared for its young.

How Did Stegosaurus Protect Itself?

Stegosaurus's best defense was its powerful tail, which anchored two pairs of deadly spikes, each about two feet long. With a quick push sideways with its front legs, the stegosaurus could pivot and keep its flexible tail pointed toward its attacker. Scientists can only guess whether stegosaurus's plates were used for defense. Some think the stegosaurus may have been able to move its sharp plates up and down, helping to ward off attacking meat-eaters. Others believe the plates were heating devices. Like modern reptiles, stegosaurus may have depended upon direct sunlight to warm itself. Stegosaurus's cold blood would have warmed up as it circulated through the single row of plates. The plates could also have worked in reverse to cool stegosaurus when the dinosaur overheated.

Why Did Stegosaurus Disappear?

Stegosaurus vanished by the early Cretaceous Period, about one hundred thirty-five million years ago—long before the sudden disappearance of all the dinosaurs. No one knows why the stegosaurus died out. Some scientists believe its fate may have had something to do with its lack of intelligence or lack of adequate protection. Climate changes or other natural forces beyond its control could also have caused its death.